ANIMORPHS
THE VISITOR

ORPHS
THE VISITOR

K.A. APPLEGATE & **MICHAEL GRANT**
A GRAPHIC NOVEL BY **CHRIS GRINE**

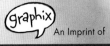
An Imprint of
◣ SCHOLASTIC

For the Animorphs fandom who've made
me feel so unbelievably welcome in your world.
I can't thank you enough.

–CG

Text copyright © 2021 by Katherine Applegate
Art copyright © 2021 by Chris Grine

All rights reserved. Published by Graphix, an imprint of Scholastic Inc.,
Publishers since 1920. SCHOLASTIC, GRAPHIX, ANIMORPHS, and associated
logos are trademarks and/or registered trademarks of Scholastic Inc.

The publisher does not have any control over and does not assume any
responsibility for author or third-party websites or their content.

No part of this publication may be reproduced, stored in a retrieval system,
or transmitted in any form or by any means, electronic, mechanical,
photocopying, recording, or otherwise, without written permission of the
publisher. For information regarding permission, write to Scholastic Inc.,
Attention: Permissions Department, 557 Broadway, New York, NY 10012.

This book is a work of fiction. Names, characters, places, and incidents
are either the product of the author's imagination or are used fictitiously,
and any resemblance to actual persons, living or dead, business
establishments, events, or locales is entirely coincidental.

Library of Congress Control Number Available

ISBN 978-1-338-53839-7 (hardcover)
ISBN 978-1-338-53837-3 (paperback)

10 9 8 7 6 5 4 3 2 1   21 22 23 24 25

Printed in China   62
First edition, October 2021
Edited by Zack Clark
Creative Director: Phil Falco
Publisher: David Saylor

5

13

I WASN'T BEING SEXIST. IT GOES BOTH WAYS.

SEE, FROM FAR OFF, I LOOK TALLER THAN I AM, RIGHT?

YOU LOOK LIKE A FAIRLY SMART GUY, AND THEN YOU OPEN YOUR MOUTH.

MARCO, YOUR PROBLEM ISN'T WITH PEOPLE **SEEING** YOU TOO WELL, IT'S WITH PEOPLE **HEARING** YOU TOO WELL.

I DON'T KNOW ABOUT YOU GUYS, BUT I HAVE A TON OF HOMEWORK TO GET TO.

YEAH, ME TOO.

IT'S SUCH A DRAG. THE CHORES AND THE HOMEWORK ALL COME RUSHING BACK AS SOON AS WE CHANGE BACK INTO OUR BORING HUMAN SELVES.

OH... TOBIAS...

I DIDN'T MEAN...

WE SHOULD GO BEFORE IT GETS DARK.

18

THIS MORPHING THING WOULD BE SO EXCELLENT IF IT WEREN'T FOR THE WHOLE THING WITH THE YEERKS.

I MEAN, IF LIFE WAS NORMAL, WE COULD REALLY USE THESE POWERS.

TO DO WHAT? FIGHT CRIME?

FIGHT CRIME? WHO ARE YOU? SPIDER-MAN?

I'M TALKING ABOUT SHOW BUSINESS. MOVIES! TV SHOWS!

WE'D BE **HOT** IN HORROR MOVIES.

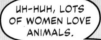

OR WHAT ABOUT STUNTPEOPLE?

ONE OF US COULD JUMP OFF THE TALLEST BUILDING AND IT WOULD BE TOTALLY REALISTIC. THEN WE JUST MORPH INTO A BIRD ON THE WAY DOWN AND FLY AWAY.

NO TRESPASSING

NOW I'M **REALLY** MAD AT THE YEERKS!

THEY'RE GETTING IN THE WAY OF MY SHOWBIZ CAREER. I COULD BE **RICH!** I COULD HAVE BEAUTIFUL SUPERMODELS ALL OVER ME.

UH-HUH, LOTS OF WOMEN LOVE ANIMALS.

BUT SOONER OR LATER YOU'D HAVE TO CHANGE BACK INTO YOUR ACTUAL SELF, MARCO.

AND THEN, BOOM, THEY'D BE OUTTA THERE.

21

ANYONE FEEL LIKE TAKING A SHORTCUT?
NO THANKS.
PRIVATE
WHAT ABOUT YOU, CASSIE?
CASSIE?
ARE YOU OKAY?

23

SOME GAME. **SOME** SPORT.

WE **DIDN'T** LOSE, ANYWAY.

I KNOW WE DIDN'T SAVE TOM, AND WE SURE DIDN'T **STOP** THE YEERKS.

BUT WE GAVE THEM A **REASON** TO BE AFRAID.

YEAH, THEY'RE TERRIFIED OF US. VISSER THREE PROBABLY CAN'T SLEEP AT NIGHT.

HE'S SO WORRIED ABOUT FIVE KIDS.

VISSER THREE DOESN'T THINK WE'RE A **THREAT**, RACHEL. HE THINKS WE'RE **LUNCH**.

HE DOESN'T KNOW WHO...OR WHAT...WE ARE.

THE YEERKS ARE **CONVINCED** THAT WE'RE ANDALITE WARRIORS BECAUSE THEY KNOW THAT WE CAN MORPH.

AND THEY KNOW THAT WE **FOUND** THE YEERK POOL, INFILTRATED IT, AND TOOK OUT A FEW OF THEIR TAXXONS AND HORK-BAJIR WHILE WE WERE AT IT.

I THINK THEY'RE PROBABLY A LITTLE NERVOUS, AT LEAST.

25

RACHEL'S RIGHT. BUT JUST THE SAME, I DON'T THINK WE WANT TO TRY TO GO BACK TO THE YEERK POOL.

BESIDES... THE DOOR'S GONE.

I JUST WANTED TO SEE IF THE DOOR STILL WORKED, OKAY? JUST IN CASE.

BUT IT'S NOT THERE ANYMORE.

SO WE FIND ANOTHER WAY TO GET AT THEM.

WE CAN FOLLOW TOM AGAIN, WHEN IT'S TIME FOR HIS YEERK TO RETURN TO THE POOL.

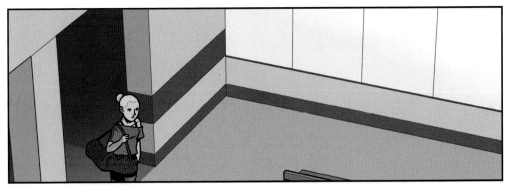

HEY, MELISSA. HOW'S IT GOING?

FINE. HOW ARE YOU?

OH, PRETTY MUCH THE SAME OLD THING.

MELISSA, I WAS THINKING...MAYBE YOU'D LIKE TO WALK OVER TO THE MALL WITH ME AFTER CLASS?

I NEED TO GRAB A NEW PAIR OF SNEAKERS.

THE **MALL**? YOU MEAN, GO SHOPPING?

YEAH. YOU KNOW, WALK AROUND AND LOOK AT STUFF? MAYBE CHECK OUT THE CUTE GUYS OR MAKE FUN OF THE SNOTTY WOMEN AT THE PERFUME COUNTERS?

I'M, UM, KIND OF BUSY.

OH. THAT'S COOL.

MELISSA, WAIT... I FEEL LIKE WE'VE KIND OF GONE IN DIFFERENT WAYS, YOU KNOW? I MISS YOU.

OKAY, WELL, MAYBE WE COULD GET TOGETHER SOMETIME.

DID HE? I WASN'T LOOKING.

IT WAS PROBABLY JUST THE RAIN.

THERE. YOU CAN TURN LEFT THERE.

OH, I KNOW WHERE **YOU** LIVE.

THANKS FOR THE RIDE, MR. CHAPMAN.

HEY, MELISSA, I WAS TOTALLY SERIOUS ABOUT US GETTING TOGETHER, OKAY?

SURE, RACHEL. ABSOLUTELY.

HEY. WHAT HAPPENED TO YOUR SHOES?

SEE? I TOLD YOU I NEEDED TO GO SHOPPING.

GOOD QUESTION.

WHAT WAS THAT, DEAR?

SHE'S FINE.

HEY, WHAT'S FOR DINNER?

PIZZA? CHINESE? ANYTHING ELSE YOU CAN ORDER OVER THE PHONE?

I'M SORRY, BUT I HAVE THIS BRIEF AND THERE'S COURT IN THE MORNING.

MOM, I LOVE YOU, BUT YOUR COOKING ISN'T ALL THAT GREAT. IT'S NO BIG DEAL ORDERING PIZZA.

WELL, AT LEAST GET SOME VEGGIES ON IT.

NO PROMISES.

DO YOU MIND IF CASSIE AND THE BOYS COME OVER?

SURE. JUST TRY TO KEEP IT DOWN.

OKAY, I SCREWED UP.

YOU **SURE** DID! YOU SCREWED UP SO--

MARCO, CHILL.

IT'S NOT RACHEL'S FAULT THAT GUY WAS HARASSING HER. I'M JUST GLAD YOU'RE SAFE.

AND I'D HAVE PAID MY NEXT **TEN** ALLOWANCES TO SEE THE LOOK ON HIS FACE.

THE IMPORTANT THING IS THAT IT DOESN'T SOUND LIKE RACHEL CAN USE MELISSA TO GET CLOSE TO CHAPMAN.

NOT IF SHE'S A CONTROLLER HERSELF. AND NOT IF SHE'S GOING TO CONTINUE BEING WEIRD TO RACHEL.

I GUESS WE'LL HAVE TO FIND ANOTHER WAY. I MEAN, WE KNOW WHERE CHAPMAN'S OFFICE IS. WE KNOW WHERE HIS HOUSE IS.

MAYBE WE COULD JUST MORPH INTO SOME SMALL ANIMALS AND HIDE OUT.

SMALL ANIMALS LIKE WHAT?

WHEN JAKE TURNED INTO A LIZARD HE GOT STEPPED ON. HE LOST HIS TAIL.

BESIDES, WHAT ARE YOU GOING TO MORPH INTO? A COCKROACH?

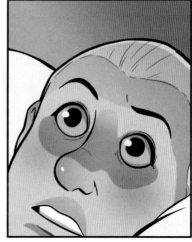

GROSS.

THE PROBLEM WITH THAT IS THE ROACHES' SENSES MIGHT NOT BE USEFUL TO US.

I MEAN, CAN THEY EVEN HEAR IN A WAY THAT WOULD MAKE IT POSSIBLE FOR US TO UNDERSTAND WHAT WE'RE HEARING?

YOU GUYS!

CAT!

WHAT ABOUT A CAT?

WHAT IS IT?

IT'S ME AND MELISSA. IT WAS HER BIRTHDAY AND WE WERE PLAYING WITH THE PRESENT HER DAD GAVE HER.

SO...?

SO...HER PRESENT WAS A CAT!

WHAT DOES THE CAT LOOK LIKE?

HIS NAME IS FLUFFER. I REMEMBER THAT MUCH.

FLUFFER MCKITTY.

SERIOUSLY?

IT'S MOSTLY BLACK AND WHITE PATCHES.

I'LL LOOK AROUND. MAYBE HE'S ALREADY OUTSIDE.

YOU KNOW WHAT WE NEED? WE NEED ANOTHER KITTY.

WE SHOULD HAVE THOUGHT OF THAT. THEN WE COULD HAVE THE SECOND CAT CALL TO FLUFFER.

MEOWFLUFFER, COME MEOWT! MEOW! COME AND PLAY MEOW!

I THINK IT'S A **GREAT** IDEA! MAYBE THE **BEST** IDEA.

RATS?

HERE? THIS IS SUBURBIA.

I MEAN, IT'S A **LOT** BETTER THAN WHERE I LIVE. THEY HAVE RATS?

THERE ARE RATS EVERYWHERE. RATS AND MICE AND ALL KINDS OF PLUMP, JUICY--

GET A GRIP, TOBIAS. DON'T START EATING RATS, ALL RIGHT?

I DON'T KNOW IF I CAN HAVE SOMEONE WHO EATS RATS FOR A FRIEND.

SHUT UP, MARCO.

I ATE A SPIDER. DOES THAT MEAN YOU AND I CAN'T BE FRIENDS?

WELL, YEAH, I GUESS YOU'RE RIGHT. BESIDES, I'VE BEEN KNOWN TO EAT EGGPLANT.

AREN'T YOU FORGETTING SOMETHING?

NOT YET. I'LL GRAB FLUFFER AND BRING HIM BACK OVER HERE.

YOU TWO STAY HERE AND TRY TO LOOK CASUAL.

HEY, JAKE, REMEMBER WHEN YOU WERE A LIZARD AND YOUR **TAIL** FELL OFF ON THE FLOOR?

UH, YEAH. WHY?

AND REMEMBER HOW YOU MORPHED BACK A FEW MINUTES LATER?

YES, MARCO. WHAT'S YOUR POINT?

WELL, WEREN'T YOU **WORRIED** THAT WHEN YOU MORPHED BACK YOU MIGHT NOT HAVE BUTT CHEEKS OR SOMETHING?

THERE HE IS.

I SEE HIM. HEY, FLUFFER.

HERE, KITTY KITTY.

REMEMBER ME?

HEY, FLUFFER FLUFFER. IT'S ME, RACHEL.

HE'S A MALE TOMCAT?

PLEASE TELL ME HE'S BEEN FIXED, AT LEAST.

HAVE YOU BEEN FIXED, FLUFFER MCKITTY?

WHY DO WE CARE?

BECAUSE POUND FOR POUND, A TOMCAT IS, LIKE, ONE OF THE TOUGHEST, MOST DANGEROUS LITTLE THINGS AROUND.

EVEN IF HE IS FIXED, A MALE CAT, OUT AT NIGHT IN HUNTING MODE? WE SHOULD HAVE WORN GLOVES.

WHO, MY LITTLE FRIEND FLUFFER?

HEY, RACHEL. I DON'T THINK THAT CAT REMEMBERS YOU.

I THINK IT DOES.

THIS WAS SUPPOSED TO BE THE **EASY** PART, CASSIE.

WELL, WE HAVE A CAT IN A TREE.

WHAT NOW?

TOBIAS, ARE YOU UP THERE?

THAT'S NOT WHAT I WAS GOING TO ASK.

RIGHT ABOVE YOU. BUT I'M NOT GOING TO TRY TO SNATCH AN ANGRY TOMCAT DOWN OUT OF A TREE.

WHAT I NEED IS A MOUSE.

OKAY, LITTLE SHREW, THANKS FOR YOUR HELP. YOU CAN GO NOW.

I'M NOT SURE THIS IS A GOOD IDEA.

REALLY, JAKE? YOU'RE NOT **SURE** IT'S A GOOD IDEA FOR RACHEL TO TURN INTO A SHREW IN ORDER TO LURE A **VICIOUS** CAT DOWN FROM A TREE SO SHE CAN MORPH INTO **THAT** CAT AND SNEAK INTO THE ASSISTANT PRINCIPAL'S HOUSE? WHAT **WORRIES** YOU ABOUT THAT PLAN?

YOU KNOW, RACHEL, USUALLY A CAT WILL PLAY WITH A MOUSE A LITTLE BIT.

BUT SOMETIMES THEY DON'T. SOMETIMES THEY GO RIGHT FOR THE NECK BITE.

THE MOUSE... OR THE SHREW... DIES INSTANTLY.

BE CAREFUL, RACHEL. I'LL BE WATCHING, BUT BE CAREFUL.

I DON'T WANT ANYTHING TO HAPPEN TO YOU.

OKAY, LET'S DO THIS.

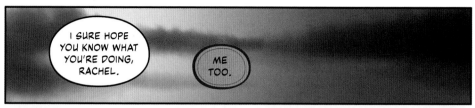

I SURE HOPE YOU KNOW WHAT YOU'RE DOING, RACHEL.

ME TOO.

THIS MAY NOT BE THE BEST IDEA I'VE EVER HAD.

FEELING KIND OF VULNERABLE OVER HERE.

HE **SEES** YOU, RACHEL.

HE FOR SURE SEES YOU. BE CAREFUL.

YOU GUYS HAD BETTER BACK OFF A LITTLE.

NOT TOO FAR. WE HAVE TO BE ABLE TO GET BETWEEN YOU AND FLUFFER FAST.

OH, I CAN KICK FLUFFER'S BUTT.

UH-HUH. CAT VERSUS MOUSE. WHO WOULD YOU BET ON?

BASED ON ALL THE CAT-AND-MOUSE CARTOONS I'VE EVER SEEN? DEFINITELY THE MOUSE.

WELL, THAT WASN'T SO HARD, I GUESS.

UGH!

I'M **NEVER** DOING THAT MORPH AGAIN.

I SHOULD HAVE DONE IT. I SHOULD HAVE USED MY LIZARD MORPH TO LURE THE CAT DOWN.

NO. THAT FREAKED YOU OUT.

I'M JUST TIRED. LET ME ACQUIRE THIS PAIN-IN-THE-BUTT CAT AND GET ON WITH THIS.

ARE YOU STILL UP FOR IT?

I SHOULDN'T HAVE LET YOU DO THE MOUSE. SHREW. WHATEVER.

IT WAS **MY** IDEA, RIGHT? BESIDES, SINCE WHEN DO YOU **LET** ME DO ANYTHING?

LET'S SEE HOW FLUFFER LIKES ME NOW THAT I'M BIGGER THAN HE IS.

HEY, BUDDY. CALM DOWN. I'M NOT GOING TO HURT YOU.

WHAT?

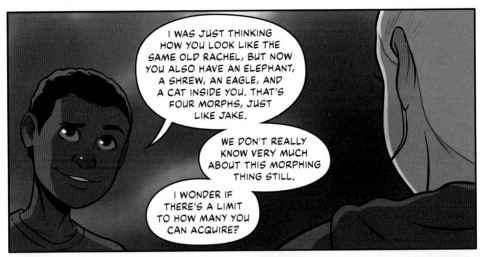

I WAS JUST THINKING HOW YOU LOOK LIKE THE SAME OLD RACHEL, BUT NOW YOU ALSO HAVE AN ELEPHANT, A SHREW, AN EAGLE, AND A CAT INSIDE YOU. THAT'S FOUR MORPHS, JUST LIKE JAKE.

WE DON'T REALLY KNOW VERY MUCH ABOUT THIS MORPHING THING STILL.

I WONDER IF THERE'S A LIMIT TO HOW MANY YOU CAN ACQUIRE?

I GUESS WE'LL FIND OUT, AND PROBABLY AT THE WORST POSSIBLE TIME.

OKAY, GUYS...I'VE ACQUIRED FLUFFER NOW. BUT MAYBE WE SHOULD DO THE **REST** OF THIS TOMORROW NIGHT?

I'M...I DON'T KNOW IF I'M AT MY **BEST** RIGHT NOW.

ANOTHER NIGHT.

I GUESS WE CAN LET FLUFFER GO NOW.

71

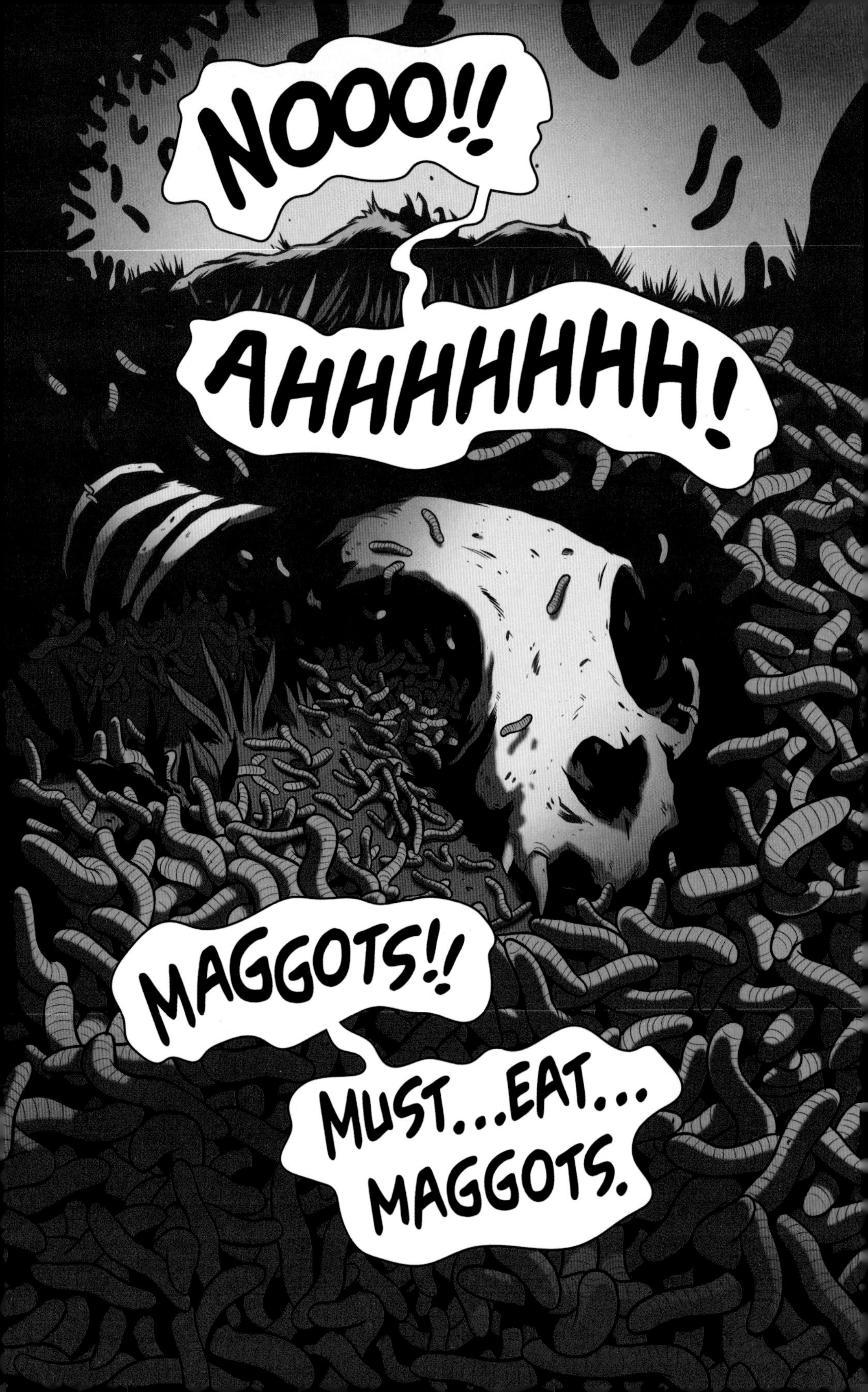
NOOO!!
AHHHHHHH!
MAGGOTS!!
MUST...EAT...
MAGGOTS.

CRUNCH
CRUNCH
CRUNCH
SQUISH
SMACK
CRUNCH
RACHEL!
RACHEL!
WAKE UP, RACHEL, WAKE UP!

BLARRGH

ARE YOU ALL RIGHT, RACHEL?

I BETTER GET MOM.

NO. NO, I'M FINE, JORDAN.

beans

DON'T WAKE UP MOM.

I'M OKAY, JUST A BAD DREAM. I GUESS IT MADE ME KIND OF SICK IS ALL. BUT I'M FINE NOW.

MUST HAVE BEEN SOME DREAM.

PSHHHHH

I GUESS SO. I CAN'T EVEN REMEMBER IT NOW. YOU KNOW HOW IT IS.

DREAMS FADE AWAY SO YOU CAN'T REMEMBER THEM.

I CAN'T BELIEVE YOU WOULD JUST **FORGET** A DREAM THAT MADE YOU SCREAM AND HURL.

I'VE NEVER BEEN VERY GOOD AT REMEMBERING DREAMS.

YOU BETTER GET BACK TO BED.

I KNOW I'M JUST YOUR LITTLE SISTER BY TWO YEARS, BUT YOU WOULD **TELL** ME IF SOMETHING BAD WAS HAPPENING TO YOU, RIGHT?

I MEAN, I WOULDN'T TELL MOM OR ANYONE. YOU COULD TRUST ME.

I KNOW I CAN TRUST YOU. IF ANYTHING BAD WAS GOING ON, I'D TELL YOU.

GOOD NIGHT. THANKS FOR SAVING ME FROM THAT NIGHTMARE. WHATEVER IT WAS.

YOU'RE THE BEST.

NIGHTMARES?

NIGHTMARES?

OH YEAH, DEFINITELY.

WHEN I MORPHED THE TIGER I HAD DREAMS, TOO, BUT NOT NIGHTMARES.

WHAT KIND OF DREAMS?

KIND OF COOL, REALLY. STALKING THROUGH A DARK FOREST AT NIGHT. I WAS HUNTING SOMETHING. IT WAS LIKE I WANTED TO CATCH IT, BUT AT THE SAME TIME IT WAS LIKE IF I DIDN'T CATCH IT THAT WOULD BE OKAY, TOO.

BECAUSE JUST RUNNING AND CREEPING AND THEN RUNNING SOME MORE THROUGH THE WOODS WAS THE BEST THING IN THE WORLD.

I FELT LIKE THAT AFTER THE ELEPHANT MORPH. IT WAS THIS INCREDIBLE FEELING OF BEING HUGE AND INVINCIBLE. LIKE I COULD NEVER EVEN POSSIBLY BE AFRAID OF ANYTHING.

BUT THE SHREW WAS DIFFERENT, WASN'T IT?

SAME WITH THE LIZARD.

ARE YOU SURE YOU'RE READY, RACHEL?

YOU CAN PUT THIS OFF IF YOU WANT. WE DON'T HAVE TO DO IT **TONIGHT**.

THE SOONER THE BETTER. WE ALL KNOW SOMETHING'S WRONG IN THAT HOUSE.

MELISSA IS STILL MY FRIEND. MAYBE SOMEHOW I CAN HELP HER.

YOUR JOB ISN'T TO HELP MELISSA. YOU'RE SUPPOSED TO BE SPYING ON CHAPMAN.

YOU'RE SUPPOSED TO BE FINDING SOME WAY FOR US TO STRIKE AT THE YEERKS SO THAT WE CAN ALL TURN INTO WILD ANIMALS AND GET OURSELVES KILLED.

I KNOW WHY I'M DOING THIS, MARCO.

WELL, TAKE CARE OF YOURSELF IN THERE. THAT'S AN ASSISTANT PRINCIPAL YOU'RE DEALING WITH.

IF HE FINDS OUT YOU'VE TURNED INTO A CAT AND ARE SNEAKING AROUND HIS HOUSE, YOU'LL GET DETENTION FOR, LIKE, A YEAR.

HOW DOES IT LOOK UP THERE, TOBIAS?

ALL CLEAR.

THE CAT'S NOWHERE NEAR THE HOUSE.

THERE'RE A COUPLE OF CARS BUT NOT COMING TOWARD YOU.

YOU KNOW, YOU HAVE QUITE A FUTURE IN BURGLARY.

YOU AND I CAN BURGLARIZE PLACES, AND JAKE CAN BE SPIDER-MAAAAAOH MYGAH!!

WHUT, MEOWRCO?

A FEW MINUTES LATER

WHOA! SUDDENLY IT ISN'T NIGHTTIME ANYMORE! I MEAN, WOW. TALK ABOUT NIGHT VISION!

A CAT'S VISION AT NIGHT IS ABOUT EIGHT TIMES STRONGER THAN A HUMAN'S.

EIGHT TIMES? NOT SEVEN, OR EVEN NINE? HOW DO THEY EVEN MEASURE THAT?

HUSH, MARCO.

SORRY.

I FEEL TOUGH, LIKE LIQUID STEEL.

HISSSS

OKAY...SO...
JUST STARING AT A
TV THAT'S NOT EVEN
ON. NOTHING WEIRD
GOING ON HERE.

BEEP
BEEP

...DIVIDED BY
THE SQUARE ROOT...
NO, WAIT, NO, SQUARE
ROOT TIMES...IS
THAT RIGHT?

MELISSA.

93

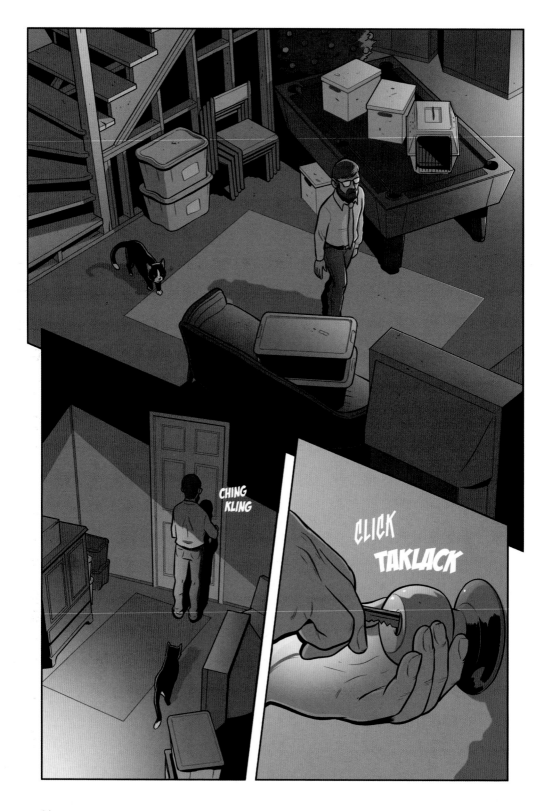

97

THE COUNCIL OF THIRTEEN WILL HEAR OF IT. THEY WILL WONDER WHY I REPORTED TO THEM THAT ALL THE ANDALITE SHIPS NEAR THIS PLANET HAD BEEN DESTROYED AND ALL THE ANDALITES KILLED. THEY WILL BE **SUSPICIOUS.** THEY WILL BE **ANGRY.** AND WHEN THE COUNCIL OF THIRTEEN IS ANGRY WITH **ME,** I AM ANGRY WITH **YOU.**

WHAT IS THAT?

WHAT? OH... OH, THAT.

UH-OH!

LOOK CASUAL, RACHEL. DON'T FREAK OUT.

IT'S CALLED A CAT. IT'S AN EARTH SPECIES USED AS A PET.

THE HUMANS KEEP THEM CLOSE AND FIND COMFORT IN THEM.

WHY IS IT IN HERE?

IT BELONGS TO THE GIRL. MY...THE HOST'S DAUGHTER.

I SEE. WELL, KILL IT. KILL IT IMMEDIATELY.

DON'T MOVE A WHISKER.

VERY WELL. DO NOT VIOLATE YOUR COVER OR DRAW ATTENTION.

WHAT IS IT DOING NOW?

IT'S MERELY SIGNALING THAT IT WISHES TO BE FED.

INTERESTING. CLAWS, TEETH, AND FEROCITY MIXED WITH THE SUBTLETY TO MANIPULATE CREATURES LARGER THAN ITSELF. A WORTHY CREATURE.

LET IT LIVE UNTIL WE HAVE RESOLVED THE MATTER OF THE GIRL.

THE GIRL? BUT... VISSER...THE AGREEMENT WITH THE HUMAN, CHAPMAN...

AGREEMENT? DON'T BE A **FOOL!** WE MAKE AGREEMENTS TO GAIN VOLUNTARY HOSTS.

AGREEMENTS ARE A TOOL. JUST AS YOU ARE MY TOOL. IF YOU HAD BROUGHT ME THE ANDALITE BANDITS, I WOULD NOT HAVE TO CONCERN MYSELF WITH A CAT OR A GIRL.

WHAT ARE THE VISSER'S ORDERS?

HE WANTS THE ANDALITE BANDITS.

HE...HE MORPHED INTO A VANARX.

A YEERKBANE.

I'D HEARD HE ACQUIRED A VANARX, BUT I THOUGHT IT WAS JUST ANOTHER STORY TO FRIGHTEN HIS UNDERLINGS.

HE SHOWED ME... HE SHOWED ME HOW HE DESTROYED INISS ONE-SEVEN-FOUR.

HE USED A VANARX ON AN INISS OF THE SECOND CENTURY?

YOU ONLY HAVE TEN MINUTES TO SPARE, RACHEL. I HOPE IT WAS WORTH SCARING US ALL HALF TO DEATH.

DID YOU AT LEAST DISCOVER SOMETHING USEFUL?

YES, I DISCOVERED **PLENTY.** I DISCOVERED THAT CHAPMAN HAS A WAY TO COMMUNICATE DIRECTLY WITH VISSER THREE.

I DISCOVERED THAT VISSER THREE IS PRETTY HOT TO CATCH US, ALTHOUGH HE **STILL** THINKS WE'RE ANDALITES.

AND I DECIDED SOMETHING, TOO.

WHAT'S THAT?

I DECIDED THAT I DON'T CARE **WHAT** IT TAKES OR HOW MANY **RISKS** I HAVE TO RUN. I DON'T CARE WHAT HAPPENS TO ME. I HATE THE YEERKS.

I **HATE** THEM! AND I **WILL** FIND A WAY TO STOP THEM.

RACHEL, WAIT UP.

MEETING LATER, OKAY?

YEAH. WHATEVER. WHERE AT?

THE CHURCH TOWER, WHERE WE WERE THE OTHER DAY.

OKAY. BUT THAT'S A LONG WALK.

SO DON'T WALK.

MAN, GETTING THIS EAGLE BODY OFF THE GROUND IS A REAL WORKOUT.

YOU SHOULD TRY FLYING NEAR THE MALL. THERE ARE SOME GREAT THERMALS THERE.

THE MALL? WHY THE MALL?

THE CONCRETE GETS HOT IN THE SUN. THE CONCRETE, THE CARS, THE BUILDINGS THEMSELVES-- THEY'RE ALL HOT. SO THERE'S ALMOST ALWAYS A NICE, WARM UPDRAFT.

FLYING IS THE NICEST THING IN THE WORLD.

IT'S ONE OF THE NICEST THINGS. BUT THERE ARE THINGS YOU MISS, TOO.

THERE'S THE CHURCH TOWER. I SEE ANOTHER BIRD HEADING TOWARD IT. AND I THINK I SEE CASSIE COMING OUT OF HER MORPH.

DOWN WE GO.

SHORTLY

YOU KNOW WHAT WE NEED?

NACHOS?

NO, JAKE.

WE NEED TO COORDINATE THESE MORPHING OUTFITS.

RACHEL'S STYLISH, AS ALWAYS.

PUT IT ALL TOGETHER AND WE LOOK PRETTY SCRUFFY.

I MEAN, CASSIE'S WEARING GREEN AND PURPLE, AND JAKE'S GOT ON THOSE **AWFUL** BIKE SHORTS.

WHAT DO YOU WANT, MARCO? FOR US ALL TO WEAR BLUE WITH A BIG NUMBER FOUR ON OUR CHESTS?

BECOME THE FANTASTIC FOUR?

THE FANTASTIC FOUR **PLUS** THE AMAZING BIRD BOY.

NO WAY. I'M THINKING MORE AN X-MEN KIND OF THING. IT'S NOT ABOUT BEING IDENTICAL--IT'S JUST ABOUT HAVING SOME STYLE. RIGHT NOW, IF ANYONE SAW US, THEY WOULDN'T THINK, "OH, COOL, SUPERHEROES." THEY'D THINK, "MAN, THOSE PEOPLE DO **NOT** KNOW HOW TO DRESS."

MARCO, I THINK IT'S TIME TO GET OVER THIS FANTASY OF YOURS. WE **AREN'T** SUPERHEROES. THIS **ISN'T** A COMIC BOOK.

YES, BUT I REALLY, REALLY **WANT** IT TO BE A COMIC BOOK. SEE, IN A COMIC BOOK, THE HEROES **DON'T** GET KILLED.

I MEAN, OKAY, THEY GET KILLED; BUT USUALLY NOT THE **BIG** ONES. OR IT'S **ONLY** TEMPORARY.

CAN WE DEAL WITH REALITY HERE?

WE HAVE BUSINESS TO DISCUSS.

WHAT'S THE MATTER WITH GREEN AND PURPLE?

IT'S A **MAJOR** FASHION NO-NO.

BEEN READING LOTS OF FASHION MAGAZINES, MARCO?

PEOPLE? AND I USE THE TERM LOOSELY. WE **NEED** TO DECIDE WHAT WE'RE DOING HERE.

I WANT TO DECIDE WHAT WE'RE **NOT** DOING NEXT.

I SHOULD BE SPENDING MORE TIME WITH MY DAD.

HE'S STILL... MESSED UP OVER MY MOM...SINCE... SHE DROWNED.

DON'T **EVER** LET ANY OF THIS GET IN THE WAY OF SPENDING TIME WITH YOUR DAD.

HE **NEEDS** YOU. WE NEED YOU, TOO, MARCO, BUT YOUR DAD COMES FIRST.

WHY? WE LEARNED A LOT ALREADY. WE--

WE DIDN'T LEARN THE LOCATION OF THE KANDRONA.

THAT'S WHAT WE NEED TO DO, SOONER OR LATER.

THE ANDALITE MADE IT PRETTY CLEAR TO TOBIAS THAT THE KANDRONA IS A WEAK POINT FOR THE YEERKS. IF WE DESTROY THAT, WE HURT THEM BAD.

EXCUSE ME, RACHEL, BUT WHAT IS A KANDRONA?

I MEAN, WE KNOW WHAT IT DOES, BUT WHAT DOES IT LOOK LIKE?

HOW BIG IS IT?

FOR ALL WE KNOW, THE KANDRONA COULD BE THE SIZE OF A LIGHTER AND BE IN VISSER THREE'S POCKET.

THAT'S NOT THE IMPRESSION I GOT FROM THE ANDALITE.

WHATEVER. THE POINT IS, HOW DO WE DESTROY SOMETHING WHEN WE DON'T EVEN KNOW WHAT IT IS?

THAT'S WHY WE HAVE TO FOLLOW OUR ONE LEAD.

CHAPMAN. CHAPMAN COMMUNICATES WITH VISSER THREE. THE TWO OF THEM KNOW WHERE THE KANDRONA IS.

IF I SPY ON THEM, MAYBE I CAN FIGURE IT OUT.

I DON'T THINK YOU SHOULD GO BACK IN THERE ALONE.

HOW IS ANYONE ELSE GOING TO GO IN WITH ME?

WE CAN'T HAVE TWO CATS RUNNING AROUND. AS FLUFFER, I CAN GO ANYWHERE WITHOUT ANY OF THEM BEING SUSPICIOUS.

EXCUSE ME? YOU MORPHED INTO A FLEA? A **FLEA?!**

YEAH. I'M ON YOUR BACK. OR YOUR HEAD? I CAN'T TELL.

I DON'T REALLY HAVE EYES. AT LEAST NOT EYES THAT SEE ANYTHING I CAN UNDERSTAND. ALL I KNOW IS WARM OR NOT WARM. I...I THINK I CAN SMELL BLOOD.

THAT'S ABOUT IT. AND I CAN KIND OF SENSE MOTION. LIKE WHEN YOUR HAIR STOOD UP, I KNEW THERE WAS SOMETHING GOING ON AROUND ME.

JAKE, THIS IS SICK. THIS IS BEYOND SICK. WHAT IS THE MATTER WITH YOU? A FLEA? ARE YOU INSANE?

JUST BEING A LIZARD MADE YOU SICK. THIS IS WAY WORSE.

TAK
TAK
TAK

ACTUALLY IT'S NOT SO BAD. I DON'T KNOW HOW TO EXPLAIN IT, BUT THE FLEA MIND IS SO LIMITED. IT'S EASY TO CONTROL. ALL IT KNOWS IS TO MOVE TOWARD THE SENSE OF BLOOD AND EAT.

I EXPECTED IT TO BE HORRIBLE, BUT WHEN CASSIE AND MARCO AND I TESTED IT OUT--

THEY'RE IN ON THIS WITH YOU?

REPORT, INISS TWO-TWO-SIX. I HOPE FOR YOUR SAKE THAT YOU HAVE GOOD NEWS.

I HAVE FOUR NEW VOLUNTARY HOSTS, VISSER.

TWO ARE CHILDREN RECRUITED THROUGH OUR FRONT ORGANIZATION, THE SHARING.

OF THE TWO ADULTS, ONE IS AN AGENT OF THE FBI, A SORT OF POLICEMAN. HE MAY BE VERY--

FOOL!

DO YOU THINK I CARE ABOUT A HANDFUL OF HOSTS?

WHAT HAVE YOU LEARNED OF THE ANDALITE BANDITS?

VISSER, WHAT CAN I DO...

UNLESS THEY **SHOW** THEMSELVES?

THEY USED VERY POWERFUL, DANGEROUS EARTH ANIMALS IN THE ATTACK ON THE POOL.

FIND OUT HOW THEY OBTAINED SUCH MORPHS.

YES, VISSER. I WILL DO--

YES. YOU WILL. AND WE HAVE ANOTHER MATTER.

WE NEED SIX MORE HUMAN-CONTROLLERS, SUITABLE FOR WORK AS GUARDS.

THEY'LL BE USED TO INCREASE THE SECURITY AROUND THE KANDRONA.

WHAT'S HAPPENING?

CHAPMAN'S GETTING REAMED BY VISSER THREE.

TOO BAD MARCO ISN'T HERE. HE'D ENJOY SEEING CHAPMAN GET CHEWED OUT.

VISSER THREE WANTS US BAD.

OR AT LEAST HE WANTS THE ANDALITES HE THINKS WE ARE.

HE'S PUTTING EXTRA GUARDS AROUND THE KANDRONA.

HUMAN-CONTROLLERS.

146

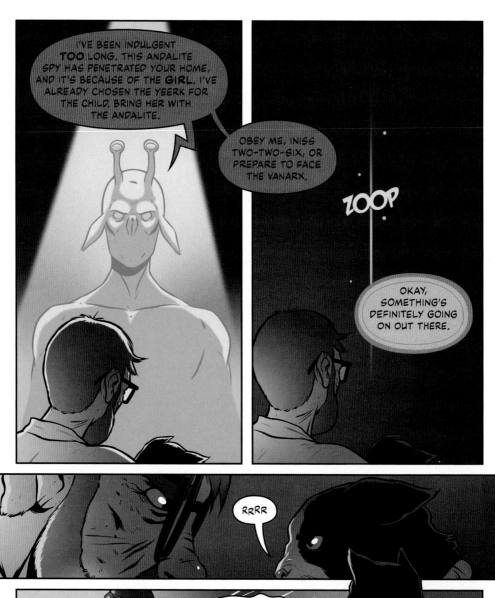

BWOOP

GET DOWN HERE!

NOW!

OH. THIS IS BAD.

IT GETS WORSE. VISSER THREE WANTS MELISSA, **TOO**.

JUST KEEP YOUR DISTANCE, ANDALITE, OR I'LL **FRY** YOU.

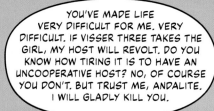

YOU'VE MADE LIFE VERY DIFFICULT FOR ME. VERY DIFFICULT. IF VISSER THREE TAKES THE GIRL, MY HOST WILL REVOLT. DO YOU KNOW HOW TIRING IT IS TO HAVE AN UNCOOPERATIVE HOST? NO, OF COURSE YOU DON'T. BUT TRUST ME, ANDALITE. I WILL GLADLY KILL YOU.

WHAT IS IT?

THIS **CAT** IS ONE OF THE ANDALITE BANDITS.

VISSER THREE WANTS HIM. GET ME THE CAGE WE USE TO TAKE HIM TO THE VET.

WHAT'S HAPPENING?

THEY'RE PUTTING ME IN A CAGE.

WHAT DO WE DO NOW?

I HAVE TO GO MEET THE VISSER.

NOW GO GET...

UNGH!

GO...GET... THE...GIRL...

UNGH!

clunk

CLACK

HE IS... URGH...

HE IS... FIGHTING ME...

HOST REBELLION.

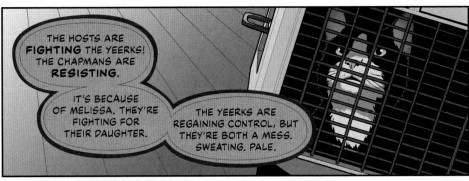

THE HOSTS ARE **FIGHTING** THE YEERKS! THE CHAPMANS ARE **RESISTING.**

IT'S BECAUSE OF MELISSA. THEY'RE FIGHTING FOR THEIR DAUGHTER.

THE YEERKS ARE REGAINING CONTROL, BUT THEY'RE BOTH A MESS. SWEATING. PALE.

I HAVE CONTROL AGAIN.

YES. BUT JUST BARELY.

THEY FIGHT FIERCELY FOR THEIR CHILDREN, THESE HUMANS.

I **CAN'T** MAINTAIN MY COVER WITH THIS HOST **WAITING** TO **ATTACK** AT **EVERY** OPPORTUNITY. I HAVE TO BE AT SCHOOL. HE'S EXHAUSTED FOR NOW, BUT HE **WILL** STRIKE AGAIN. HE KNOWS HE CAN'T WIN.

HE DOESN'T HAVE TO **WIN.**

ALL HE HAS TO DO IS WAIT UNTIL YOU ARE IN A MEETING WITH PARENTS OR MEMBERS OF THE SCHOOL BOARD, THEN STRIKE.

THEY'LL THINK YOU'VE LOST YOUR MIND.

ANDALITE SCUM!

BOOT

I'LL TAKE THE ANDALITE TO VISSER THREE. MAYBE...MAYBE I CAN MAKE HIM UNDERSTAND.

GO, QUICKLY.

I WILL.

DADDY?

DADDY? WHAT ARE YOU DOING?

DADDY?

DO YOU HAVE FLUFFER IN THERE?

IT'S MELISSA.

IF SHE DOESN'T BACK OFF, SHE'S GOING TO FORCE THEM TO TAKE HER!

DADDY, WAIT!

159

THUNK

SO...WHEREVER IT IS WE'RE GOING, I THINK WE MIGHT BE THERE.

JAKE, WE'RE TRAPPED. HE'S GOT A DRACON BEAM AND I'M IN A CAGE.

I **CAN'T** MORPH BACK OR THEY'LL SEE I'M HUMAN.

CHAPMAN WILL RECOGNIZE ME, AND HOW LONG DO YOU THINK IT WILL TAKE THEM TO FIGURE OUT WHO THE **REST** OF YOU ARE?

IT WOULD BE THE END.

YOU KNOW I'M RIGHT, JAKE.

YES, THAT ALL SOUNDS VERY DRAMATIC, RACHEL, BUT WE'RE NOT BEATEN YET.

THE ONLY HOPE IS FOR ME TO STAY IN CAT MORPH.

THEY'LL PROBABLY... YOU KNOW. BUT AT LEAST THEY'LL NEVER FIND OUT ABOUT THE REST OF YOU.

TIME TO MEET THE VISSER, ANDALITE. HE'LL HAVE A WONDERFUL TIME WITH YOU.

UH-OH. WE'RE AT THE CONSTRUCTION SITE, JAKE.

YOU HAVE TO GET OUT OF HERE!

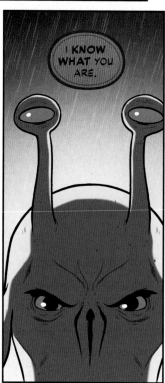

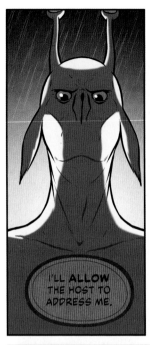

175

THE HOST WILL ATTEMPT TO DISRUPT YOU?

YES, VISSER. THE WOMAN AS WELL.

SHE IS NOT AS STRONG AS THIS ONE, BUT SHE WAS ABLE TO GAIN CONTROL OF ONE HAND. PERHAPS SHE HAS DEEPER STRENGTHS THAN WE KNEW. I'M OF MORE USE WITH A PASSIVE, VOLUNTARY HOST. BUT I'M YOUR TOOL, VISSER. I WILL DO AS YOU COMMAND.

YES, YOU WILL CERTAINLY DO AS I COMMAND.

LUCKILY, YOU'VE BROUGHT ME THE ANDALITE BANDIT, AND THIS WILL OCCUPY MY TIME FOR A LITTLE WHILE.

LEAVE THE GIRL FOR NOW.

NOW GET OUT.

YOU TEST MY PATIENCE.

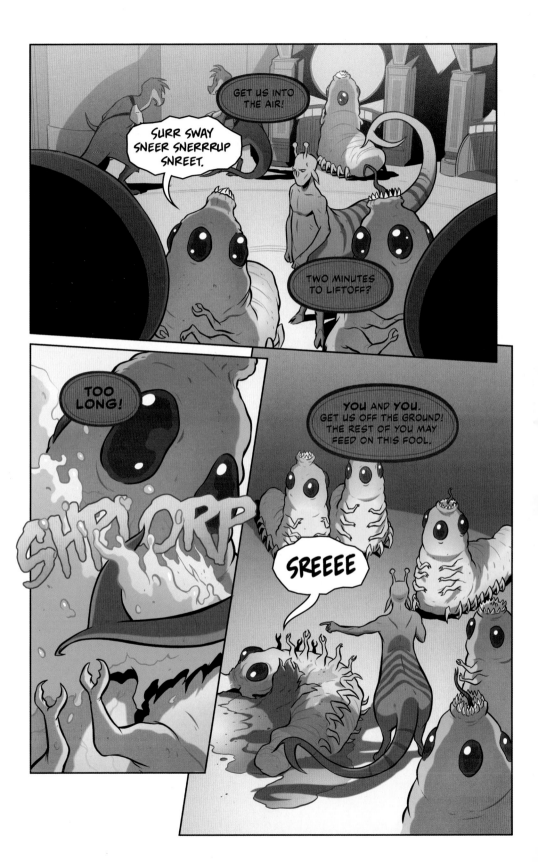

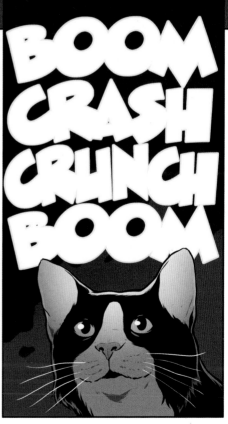

195

RACHEL, ARE YOU OKAY?

I'M FINE, TOBIAS.

THANKS TO YOU.

WHAT ABOUT JAKE?

THE OTHERS?

DID THEY MAKE IT?

THEY'RE ALL FINE. MARCO GOT HIS FEATHERS A LITTLE SINGED, BUT HE'S OKAY. CASSIE, TOO.

FLUMPH

K. A. APPLEGATE is the married writing team Katherine Applegate and Michael Grant. Their Animorphs™ series has sold millions of copies worldwide and alerted the world to the presence of the Yeerks. Katherine is also the author of the Endling series and the Newbery Medal–winning *The One and Only Ivan*. Michael is also the author of the Front Lines and Gone series.

CHRIS GRINE is the creator of Chickenhare and *Time Shifters*. He's been making up stories since he was a kid, and not just to get out of trouble with his parents. Nowadays, Chris spends most of his time writing and illustrating books, drinking lots of coffee, and sleeping as little as possible. He spends his free time with his wife, playing with his kids, watching movies, and collecting action figures (but only the bad guys).

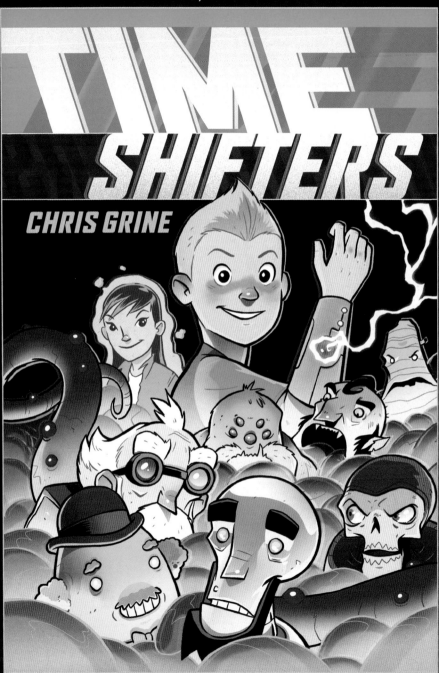

TIME SHIFTERS

CHRIS GRINE

ANIMORPHS
THE ENCOUNTER